CW01091494

A Scar of Avarice

A HANNIBAL SMYTH/ PASSING PLACE NOVELLA

MARK HAYES

Salthomle Publishing

Saltholme publishing
11 Saltholme Close
High Clarence
TS21TL

Book Layout © 2018 Saltholme publications

A Scar of Avarice / Mark Hayes -- 1st ed.
ISBN-13: 978-1717378255
ISBN-10: 1717378250

For my children; Sarah and Aaron. Neither of whom are children anymore. Both of whom have made me nothing but proud to be their father, a role to which I have seldom been suited, yet seem to have pulled off surprisingly well all the same, if by your children are you measured as a parent.

It's also for all the Blackpool Geeks…They know of whom it is that I speak.

With special thanks to Clive 'Badger' Weldon, for proofreading this, and who is therefore unable to complain about any typos he misses…

Contents

CHAPTER ONE

A scar-faced man

There is something about the British that makes them stand out amongst the crowd. Take, if you will, a boy from Kensington and put him in a bar in South Brooklyn. It doesn't matter what he's wearing, what he's drinking, or if he says a single word. Anyone with an eye keen enough for such things would know in moments he wasn't native to New York's shores. While if that casual observer were British themselves, or to be more exact, an Englishman, then even in one of the most cosmopolitan cities in the world, that Englishman would recognise one of his own, a mirror reflecting his own inner monologue.

It's something in the way they hold themselves

that's hard to quantify. An aloof prideful pomposity that conspires somehow to remain apologetic for everything they have ever done or have yet to do. It is something they are not taught, nor learn, but which is bred into them as though it seeped from the land. No matter where they are in the world, an Englishman's body language is always saying the same thing…

'We're so sorry we colonised your country in our imperial majesty, the empire was a terrible thing, glorious of course, so very, very glorious, and we gave you so much; cricket, impoverishing debt, that strange inferiority you foreigners can't help but feel when an Oxbridge accent is in the room, partition, and so many train stations, while we took all your cultural treasure back to dear old Blighty and stuck them in draws in the "Vic and Bertie". Gods it was a glorious thing the empire, bloody glorious.'

'Bloody too come to that, but you can't paint half the world pink without spilling a little red now can you? But we brought you the rule of law, habeas bloody corpus, lawyers and all that. And let's not forget parliamentary democracy because god knows that's working out so bloody well for us…'

'But, it was, of course, terrible, utterly terrible and we're so, so, so very, very sorry about all that now.'

"Sorry!"

Even in a bar that isn't in South Brooklyn, not at this exact moment at least, though the doors of Esqwith's Passing Place could not be relied upon never to open out on to Dwight Street and command a view over Coffey park. Even in a bar whose clientele was as eclectic a bunch of patrons as it was possible to have.

And so when a man, who later claimed to be known by the ponderous moniker; Hannibal Smyth entered the main bar and crossed it to sit at one of the smaller tables near the piano, Richard, the piano player, innately recognised him as a fellow subject of her majesty the Queen. Though of which Queen, in particular, was something yet to be determined…

There were, it has to be admitted, other clues beyond pure British empathy.

For instance, the man was wearing a red broadcloth coat of a military style, and dark blue trousers with what would once have been twin white piping down the side. This was a bit of a giveaway. Only the British had a tradition of red uniforms for servicemen. A tradition which spoke of the mentality of the former imperial power. It was not enough to bully the world into submission in their eyes, you had to make damn sure they saw you doing it into the bargain…

The uniform was well worn, in a way which suggested both it and its owner had seen active service of late. Which should, by all rights, have struck Richard as odd. In these latter days, indeed since before the days of Passchendaele and Ypres, even British bull-headedness had long since resigned the traditional reds' to dress uniform only.

The last time a British red coat was seen on a battlefield was around the time Michael Cane and co. faced down the Zulu nation at Rourke's Drift, or at least, the small force of men of the 24th foot proved that the combination of British grit and determination could win out against impossible odds.

Provided, of course, the small force had actual guns, and the enemies were armed with nothing more than spears and hide shields. The latter party, the Zulu's, were reputedly surprised to learn that their shields did little to slow the progress of a bullet from a seven grooved rifle barrel…

That the worry-worn look of the uniform did not strike Richard as odd, spoke somewhat of how his thinking had come to adjust to the uncanny nature of his new gig. What would once have stuck out as a little odd, if not downright strange, now seemed passably normal, or at least unworthy of serious contemplation.

In short, it took more than a man in a battle-worn British uniform, complete with both a regimental badge and a crowned service crest for something called *E.I.C.A.N.*, complete with stitching around the crest proclaiming the words '*East India Company, 3rd Air Fleet*', to surprise the passing place's resident piano player these days. Thus a man who was, Richard's logical side told him, probably no more than a really committed cos-player, in a red uniform, seemed somewhat tame in consideration. Even if the sabre and Gatling style service revolver looked very authentic in a '*could actually kill you*' kind of way.

But to be fair, Richard had recently had a conversation with a traditionally dressed Inuit carrying a seven-foot ice-encrusted whaling spear which had been dripping blood into his drink, as the ice melted.

The eye patch and the long scar down the man's left cheek were probably no more than affectations as well, his logical side went on to reason. As for the dirty soot smears on his face, the tear in one of his epaulettes, and the pained limp that favoured his right side, where old blood on his trousers suggested a wound of some kind, well, such battle-scarred authenticity was something the average Cos-player might not think of, but it was hardly proof that he was actually an authentic British officer in Her Majesty's air fleet.

That said, another somewhat less logical side of Richard informed him that it was also ever so possible that the man was exactly what he appeared to be. A British officer from an era that never was. The less logical side of himself was one Richard chose to ignore. It saved him from asking questions he suspected he would not like the answer to, and another session of cryptic wisdom from his friend Sonny, who worked the door.

That aside, Richard's fingers felt a strange urge in his fingers to play *'Men of Harlech'*. A song he only vaguely knew from the annual viewing of the aforementioned Michael Cane film that his father insisted he and his siblings sit through back in the fallow days of his childhood. A time when British TV had only four channels and rainy spring Sundays offered stark other choices.

That itch in the fingers was a sign, he supposed, the kind of sign he was getting all too accustomed to. A sign someone was nudging things again.

He let his gaze wander for a few moments until he spied the cat, stalking across the barroom floor as if she owned the place… A growing possibility which Richard had not quite dismissed as the truth.

She let her gaze fall upon him as she stepped around a table leg and her claws skittered across the wooden tiled floor. Indeed she seemed to be paying little attention to anything else. Not that it mattered, no one was about to step on her tail or anything so crass. The universe, or at least the microcosm of a universe that was Esqwith's, would not allow it. Of that, if of few other things, Richard was sure. She never had to wind her way through the barroom, a path was always cleared for her. It was not that people moved out of her way exactly, they were just never in her way to start with. Even if that meant they had moved a moment before, for no reason that they understood.

As she got close to the piano she stopped for a moment and held his gaze, then she changed direction, flicking her tail at him, as she took a few loping steps, before hopping up onto the small table where the man with the eye-patch had seated himself. She pranced a couple of times around the edge of the table, then settled down to apparently have a nap, but not before Richard quite plainly, but clearly didn't hear her say, *'Hi Harry, good of you to pop in for a while, how was India?'*

The red-coated officer gave the cat the kind of mildly puzzled look Richard was all too familiar with, not least because he had spent a lot of time wearing that same expression of late. It was an expression which said, *'Cat's don't talk, I know cats don't talk, so I didn't hear that.'*

Regardless *'Harry'* seemed to say something to the cat, and started to stroke her in an absent-minded kind of way. For no reason that made any sense to Richard, this gave the piano player an odd pang of jealousy. He tried to push the bizarre feeling away by focusing on his playing. But even that proved to be a distracted pursuit now, not least because he found he had to stop himself from playing *'God Save the Queen'*. The original version, not the one he preferred, by the Sex Pistols.

A few bars of 'Hearts of Oak' later he gave up and dropped the key cover down on the ivories.

"Time I had a break anyway." He muttered to himself, knowing full well he was not going to the bar to ask Lyal for a coffee, but was going to find himself drawn to sit with the stranger in the red uniform. *'Sometimes,'* he found himself musing, *'it's simpler just to go along with it all, rather than fight the forces of kismet.'* It was a strangely resigned thought, born of one absolute certainty in his mind. If the cat wanted him to talk to the stranger with the eyepatch, then he was going to end up doing so, because he always ended up doing things the cat wanted him to do. Ludicrous though that idea seemed even now.

"Hi, do you mind if I sit here?" he found himself asking as he came across to the table.

The Man looked up from his duties as chief petting slave to the feline overlord, looking mildly bemused at the question, and even more mildly bemused to find himself stroking a cat, before basic British civility kicked in and he nodded, saying, "Be my guest old chap." in a Home Counties accent, before adding, almost as an after-thought, "You from the north?"

"Tadcaster…" Richard replied, then as was obligatory he added, "It's near York."

"I thought I could detect a bit of a Yorkshire twang in there. Though you seem to have lost it a little in heathen climes. Captain Hannibal Smyth, formally of her Majesty's Air-Fleet, and now…" he said, offering Richard his hand as he took on a worried expression, and left that '*and now…*' hanging in the wind. Either he didn't actually know, or he was far from certain he should say what the '*and now…*' was.

Richard clasped the stranger's hand politely, trying not to notice that Hannibal's own accent had slipped away from the home-counties as well. Then realising the man was floundering with that '*and now…*' he replied by way of a rescue. "I've been away from home a long time… My name's Richard, Richard Barrick, I play here…" he added the last, while nodding towards the piano at the centre of the room.

His having been away from home for a long time was something of an understatement, he had not been back to Yorkshire since he had first moved to the states fifteen years ago. He'd long since acquired that urbane

English accent that Americans assumed all Brits had. The one favoured recently by most of Hollywood's villains.

The accent had started out as an affectation on his part, as New York Girls seemed to like it. By the time he met and married Carrie, it had become unconscious, with only the odd Yorkshire vowel dropping in once in a while, to remind him of his roots. Yet whenever he spoke to another Englishman, the affectation tended to fall away. Accent is as much an identity as anything else, it plainly said who you were, in ways long understood in the very bones of the English. He could no more hide it, nor would he wish to when talking to a southerner, as this other gentleman clearly was, than he could hide his working class roots, or his natural suspicion of beer without a head. No one is ever more northern, than a northerner amongst southerners.

At this point, to no great surprise on Richards's part, that Jolene came sauntering from the bar with two pints of bitter on her tray, and of all things, a couple of bags of pork scratchings. The southern belle smiled at them both as she put the brown beer down in front of them, then dropped the small packets of scratchings onto the table, which she then eyed with a leery suspicion.

Jolene had definite views when it came to bar snacks and the little semi-clear packets with 'Mr Porkie's' emboss upon them had a definite un-American look to them. They were way too small for one thing…

Richard, for no real reason beyond a growing appreciation of the strange way things worked in The Passing Place, spread his gaze to the back wall of the bar. He was unsurprised to see an old-fashioned picture card hanging there with packets of pork scratchings attached, which were covering most but by no means all, of a 1970's glamour model's calendar. The type which, should the bar's punters be inclined towards scrapings of deep fried pork fat snacks, would slowly reveal the picture as the packets were bought. The tantalising possibility held before purchasers was that the model was not wearing a bikini top. Something that could only be discovered if enough packets were purchased…

It was a special kind of marketing ploy happened upon by the makers of British bar snacks years before click bait ads on social media were even a twinkle in the ad-man's eye. Proof, if nothing else, that no matter how much things change, the art of manipulating men's lechery for profit never does.

Richard would have happily sworn that the snack calendar hadn't been there a few moments before, and he would also be prepared to bet it wouldn't be there later that evening either. But for the moment at least, the tacky calendar seemed to fit decor. There suddenly seemed something very late seventies about the bar-room, it was in fact very much like the kind of bar the Sweeney would have frequented about a third of the way through an episode, before they got a set of villains in a shed up at Heathrow.

The musician within him had to fight an urge to play '*Cool for Cats*' right at that moment...

He sighed to himself and grabbed a packet of scratchings. Perception is a strange thing, all the stranger when something was messing with your perceptions. Yet it was remarkable what you could get used to, if you let yourself just go with the flow. Sometimes in the Passing Place that was all you could do.

What he found himself wondering about the most was not '*Why does this feel like a seventies bar all of a sudden?*', but *Why the seventies?*, because nothing about the man with the eye-patch and the imperial looking uniform said the seventies to him… The Eighteen Seventies perhaps…

Richard was lost for a moment in the thought, once again, that something was not quite right, and found himself fixated on the calendar for a moment as it flickered with a hint of a red glow. There was something threatening about it. Something that gave him an itchy feeling that he knew was not ready to explore.

Then in the passing of the moment, the glow and the feeling, were gone, but that mental itch remained a while. Until he could shake it off and found himself locked in conversation with the man called Hannibal.

They talked for a while, of the kinds of things two Englishmen meeting in a bar for the first time will always talk about; the offside rule, and the inability of referees to apply that rule properly in the world cup, the lack of a decent spinner in the first eleven being the downfall of the touring side again. Not to mention batting collapses, penalty shootouts and why you can't get a decent cup of tea on a train.

Richard swiftly got the impression, as the conversation wound on, that Hannibal was not entirely of the class to which his uniform professed membership. There was something of the guttersnipe hiding behind the middle-class mannerisms. Something of the east end, that slipped into his Home Counties accent when he let himself relax in company. There was also something sly about him that Richard could not quite put his finger on… A touch of the rogue, or the outright villain. Yet he found he liked the strange airman, in that way you cannot help but like a Jack the lad, thief and swindler, as long as you're not the one he is out to rob and swindle.

Then, just after Jolene arrived with a second round, Richard heard a purr of a voice which emanated from the cat shaped area of the table '*Ask Harry about his scar…*' The voice said as plain as day to him, but Hannibal did not seem to notice it. It was, however, typical of the cat's subtle approach to steering a conversation, which is to say, not subtle at all…

Richard did not have to ask which scar. The scar in question was the one below the airman's eye-patch, a small slither of livid red, which glowered at you when you met his eye. It was a relatively fresh wound, of that he had no doubt, for it was far from fully healed. It was also low enough down the man's cheek to suggest it had nothing to do with whatever incident had caused him to wear an eyepatch. Every once in a while Hannibal got the urge to scratch it, Richard could tell, and was fighting that urge either because he was in company, or the inner voice that belonged to his mother was saying '*Hannibal… If you scratch it, it won't heal…*'

Richard smiled at that thought, knowing full well the inner voice of his mother would have been saying just that to him, when another passing thought struck him.

'*Harry, now why would the cat keep calling him Harry…?*' He wondered about this to himself absently. As Hannibal finished bemoaning the lack of a decent all-rounder since Pendleton retired. The name meant nothing to Richard, but that hardly mattered, the England cricket team always lacked a decent all-rounder, generally before whoever was named retired they lacked one since the guy before. It was just the way of things.

He dismissed the whole Harry thing as just another of those little mysteries he may as well put to the back of his mind, and sought for a way to bring the subject of the scar up.

When the bemoaning lulled, Richard just took the easiest and most direct approach and asked, "How did you get that scar?"

Hannibal's hand went up to the fresh wound unconsciously, stroking at it he smiled, and after a moment replied, "Stupidity on my part can't be ruled out I suppose…" then started to tell a tale that grew tall with the telling, not at all to Richards surprise…

"I was in the Himalayas until recently, up in one of those little-forgotten valleys. I could explain how I ended up there, but that would take too long and paint me in no good light I suspect. Let's just say for reasons of state Old Iron Knickers government had seen fit to offer me the chance of redemption, if I undertook a damn fool mission. That eventually after one of two rather embarrassing mishaps, led me up there."

"For reasons of convenience, I had little choice but to accept the commission. Namely, because I found it remarkably convenient not to be strung up by the neck in the name of old Vicky's justice."

"I'll not bore you with the whys and wherefores, it was just a minor affair you understand. Let's just say I came out the wrong end of a court case due to the misfortune of having an incompetent Barrister, I mean it not like I actually meant to drop an incendiary on the Queen's dockyards, and as for the other charge, it was self-defence."

"In all seriousness, what did they expect me to do, allow the bastard to stab me? Anyway, all that aside, I found myself stuck in a Himalayan monastery up in one of those little valleys no one really knows is there, and despite all that had happened I found myself at a bit of a loose end, and a tad bored."

"Which is what happens when you're not running for your life, fighting off bastards who want to kill you, being plotted against by your own crew, shot at by bandits, shot at by your own side, arrested, imprisoned, captured by rebels and not being attacked by mad American girls with razors for fingernails. It's amazing how quickly not being under duress turns to boredom… But I digress, and so let me start again…"

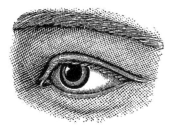

CHAPTER TWO

Aspects of Avarice

I had found myself at a monastery in a small hidden valley deep in the Himalayas. It was probably Buddhist, or Sho Lin or some other mystical, robe wearing, head shaving, bowing and scraping, cult of ancient knowledge. I don't think that really matters, do you? One of those eastern religions that get all their wisdom from old men with three-foot moustaches who sit around cross-legged all the time speaking in riddles.

You know the kind of thing 'What is the sound of one hand clapping' or 'if a tree falls in the forest and there is no one to hear it, does it get back up again...' Never quite understood it all myself.

Why is it wisdom just because it comes from far

away? If a pie and mash hawker said it on the banks of old mother Thames, you'd tell him he was talking twaddle would you not?

But if some oriental bloke said it by the side of a carp pond a thousand years ago, it's wisdom… Having spent some time in the orient I can tell you this much, there is sod all wisdom to be found when you ain't got enough rice to eat and you're growing opium in the fields…

But anyway, there was a courtyard out the back of the temple, a walled square that was used for training by the monks. Training with quite brutal looking weapons I should add. Peaceful little men in saffron robes wafting incense about is not all there is to Himalayan monasteries.

So, as I say, they had these strange and quite brutal weapons that looked exotic to my western eyes, and they moved damn fast with them. Faster than I could follow at times. Strange snake-like movements, elegant, sweeping, yet wrong at the same time. I mean gravity works the same in the mountains of the east as it does anywhere else. Fall off the side of one of those mountains sometime and you'll see what I mean… Well, briefly you will at any rate. Yet no one seemed to have told these monks that. They would leap about sometimes, hanging for moments in the air, in exactly the way people don't. Yet it seemed natural enough all the same when you watched them.

Watched them I did, for hours, but was no closer to understanding their strange drills and katas, or whatever it is they call them. A whole lot of shouting 'Hy!' while snapping their way through the same drill as everyone else, eerily in synch. That was what fascinated me most I believe, that eerie synchronicity. Twenty-odd people throwing the same punch, then the same spinning kick and punch again before an echoing resounding and perfectly together 'Hy!'. Fascinating and disturbing in equal measure.

They had a parade ground discipline that would make a drill sergeant cry with happiness if he could get her Maj's marines to keep time that closely, which I assure you, they cannot. They were not just doing this all at once, but exactly all at once. Like one body moving in disparate parts. Each the perfect mirror of the next.

Yet somehow, there was a touch of the comic about them at first viewing. Bamboo staves with hooked blades, or a couple of short staffs each less than an arm's length long, snapping in unison. I remember thinking to myself. *'They wouldn't last long against a good old volley of British guns. Sticks and hooks are no way to fight,'*

I would have said as much, had there been anyone worth talking to around…

Yet, once I'd watched them for a while, I revised my opinion. My observations left me with two distinct certainties and one aching horrible suspicion.

The first two being, that they could be very deadly with those sticks if they wished to be, and that I'd never want to face them in combat.

The latter suspicion was more of a feeling than a certainty. I got the impression that a good old volley of British guns would not do what good old fashioned volleys of British guns are supposed to do, because the monks would somehow prove to not stay in the path of a bullet long enough for it to find its mark. Which is, of course, impossible, as no one can move faster than a bullet, but I for one would not wish to test that supposition against them…

Perhaps it was simply that I found something menacing about their little drills that got under my skin. All those shouts of 'Hy!' in unison didn't help either. Chilling as they became after a while. The way they never faltered, were never less than on beat. It all had a fearsome rhythm to it...

I had, as I said, taken to watching them train all the same. It passed the morning if nothing else, and when they gathered for lunch, I would use the square myself with a training sabre, again, as much for something to do as anything else, I'll take exercise over utter boredom anytime, though I would take an afternoon in Soho getting acquainted with two of my best newly made friends over any other kind of exercise if that were an available option, I must confess.

Such delights as are easily acquired in the shadier parts of old London town were sadly unavailable to me at the time, however. The small village in the valley below was, I suspect, not a hive of indulgence and lewd behaviour... Besides which I had an eye for someone at the time, which more or less precluded investigations along those lines. Affairs of the heart you understand?

While if I am utterly honest, the thought of the short dumpy ladies of negotiable virtue wearing yak skin undergarments failed to raise my, interest, shall we say...

So a little vigorous exercise with a steel blade rather than one of another kind was really all I had to engage me.

I'd borrowed the dull little training blade from a Russian airman who spoke a broken approximation of English, which was, at least, better than my broken approximation of Russian.

Did I mention there were Russians there? No? Well there were. Russians with the nastiest looking airship I had ever seen.

There were other Europeans too, a couple of Africans and a host of Indians of every caste and creed, who belonged in that valley only slightly more than I did. But let's not digress too far. Let's just say the locals were playing 'host' for want of another word to a nefarious band of individuals.

I suspect the locals were no happier about their guests than I was to be one of them, but beyond the monks putting to test my theory on their abilities to avoid been struck with bullets, there was little they could do about it. Besides which, they were somewhat in awe of a man called Herbert who was the leader of this somewhat disparate group.

Strange name for a leader of men don't you think, '*Herbert*', it always surprised me he did not go by his middle name which was far more the kind of name you would expect of a leader. Though he chose mostly just to go by his initials, which I can understand, with a first name like Herbert. Herbert's a name for a junior officer who the staff sergeants wouldn't trust to tie his own shoelaces. Any army led by a Herbert is doomed to fail, but I digress again, and you don't really need to know my opinion of that madman.

As I said, when the monks broke for lunch I would use the square for exercise, running through my own sabre drills, against imaginary sparring partners. I was, I must admit, out of practice. In an age of airships and Howitzers, skills with a blade were generally considered much in the same way as nipple tassels in a bordello. A nice enough indulgence but by no means necessary for the bulk of the task…

Never the less, something told me getting back into

practice with naked steel may be wise. Let's just say I was not in the mountains for the air, and my rusty swordplay was something I considered it worth my time to polish, though at close quarters on an airship I would take my trusty cut-throat razor over a sabre any day of the week. Provided of course, I had the opportunity to do so from behind on a dimly lit gantry…

So practice swordplay I did, for a week or so, every afternoon for an hour while the monks ate. It felt good, to tell the truth. Working up a bit of a sweat, and using muscles which had forgotten they had jobs to do. I ached like buggery after the first day, but by the fourth, I had regained some little measure of my skill. I fenced at the academy and would have made the service team if not for… Well, let's just say skill alone is not enough to get you a place if you don't have the right surname and the kind of breeding that leads to weak chins, and a laugh like a despotic horse.

Being the bearer of a purchased commission was one thing, but it will only take you so far in the service, if your face doesn't quite fit with the Hooray Henrys.

But let's not dwell on my stunted career in old clockwork skirts armed forces. I knew going in my options were going to be limited, and given my options elsewhere outside the service I could hardly complain about my commission. Besides, a certain lack of rank has some privileges, better to be in charge of the warehouse than in charge of the man in charge of the warehouse. Leastways if you want to borrow some of its contents on an extended, never to be returned loan. There's many a junior officer who has made himself a tidy sum that way, and until my recent difficulties with Her Nibs courts, I had done quite well myself. But anyway, digressing I know…

I had managed to gather an odd audience while going through sabre drills. It was a silent one that would sit, cross-legged, eating rice from a bowl, on the edge of the courtyard, watching me each day with a disinterested eye.

I'd gathered from my own observations he was the instructor of the monks. Indeed he sat and watched them in much the same way, a subordinate shouting out instructions while he observed with an inscrutable expression. On rare occasions, he would raise a hand and say something to his assistant. This generally led to some form of dressing down or other for whomever had earned the master's dissatisfaction.

Since besides staffs and the short sticks, the monks on occasion worked with steel blades as well, I suspected the master was observing my own swordplay. I had a fancy he was a little taken by my technique. Though his expression never changed, so it was hard to judge, but I assumed, in my own vanity, that he recognised a skilled bladesmith in me.

I also got the impression, from the dedicated way in which he studied me, that he was determining how best to disarm me. Or perhaps just to get beyond my guard. It would be what I was doing, truth be told. Though I would never have spent so long at the endeavour. The way he watched with silent concentration began to worry me slightly at first. It was unnerving how little he moved. After the first few of days of this, I determined to just ignore him and focus on the task at hand.

'If he wants to watch me train, let him,' I thought to myself, while adding in my arrogance, *'perhaps he'll pick up a pointer or two of good old British swordplay.'* It had been some time since I practised my drills it has to be said, but I remained a fair hand with a sabre.

I used to be better with an epee, it is true, but there is little call for epees in actual combat. So after I graduated from the academy, and the opportunities to embarrass my classmates with a swift reposte had dried up, I trained mainly with sabre. The heavier curved single-edged sword being, as it were, more suitable for actually hacking people to death when they were trying to kill you, which is sort of the point of these things after all.

Not that I'd found the need to use my skills in actual combat. I had managed to skillfully avoid being posted anywhere near any actual conflict zones over the years. The occasional judicious backhander in the clerk's office to move your name from one list to another is not, as they claimed at my trial, an act of cowardice, but an act in line with the finest traditions of the British officer classes.

To wit, wearing a smart uniform, looking gallant and occasionally rakish, eating fine regimental dinners, sweeping debutants off their feet in the ballroom, and if at all possible onto their backs in the bedroom. All the while making damn sure other people did all of the acctual fighting, let alone any actual dying for Queen and country.

What was the point of wearing a smart uniform after all, if one was not alive to have the medals pinned upon it?

Of course as a junior officer of little social standing, avoiding being sent into combat was a little more challenging than it was for the Eton Hoorays. Bribery was an expensive matter, and beyond my meagre salary, but a skilled man with the right kind of moral centre can always find ways to supplement his salary, and all those regular patrol flights are so useful for moving a little contraband from here to there, so long as you don't make the mistake of getting caught.

Or, as a random example, throwing someone out of the bomb bay doors who wants to cut you out of the deal, to take a larger slice of the pie for himself.

'He was trying to kill me, your honour, it was self-defence, honest it was…'

I would also offer this advice. If you're relying on the defence of self-defence, make sure the man you're throwing out of the bomb bay doors doesn't, inexplicitly, happen to have a couple of phosphorus flares in his pockets. The kind that burn at a thousand degrees.

Further to this, if you do happen to do so, given you really had no choice but to defend yourself against a man whom the court can annoyingly prove was your partner in a little judicious smuggling. I advise most strongly you don't do this right on top of the biggest munitions dump in South East England…

The unforgiving courts of old Iron Buns are somewhat more unforgiving than usual of those chaps that blow up her dockyards.

All that was behind me now. Of course, it was behind me in the way a man with a knife can be said to be behind you, but behind me none the less. And I digress a little. Let's just say that had I been holding a sabre at the time I fancy much of what had befallen me since could have been avoided. For all my faults I remain more than a little proud of my ability with the airman's blade. I suspect that, had I been holding one, negotiations with Hardacre, the petty thief who got me into this mess to start with due to his avarice, would have been much smoother. But we all have regrets…

Proud though I was of my ability with a sabre, I was horribly aware of one thing while I went through my drills in the training square. My new blind spot. The very literal one. My left eye, or rather the lack of it.

You've noted my patch I am sure, well let's just say that is a rather long story involving a spider of a kind and a mad grimy little scientist with jam jars for spectacles and all the personal warmth of a wet lettuce called William Gates. That and the machinations of the Ministry…

Which ministry you ask?

The Ministry, and if you need to ask again, then let's just say you're better off not knowing. Either way, I'll not go into it right now, but it had left me somewhat one-sided in the vision department because the alternative had been somewhat worse.

At first, I tried to compensate for the lack of vision from my left side. But trying to keep to my right, placed me off balance and felt wrong. These were just training drills after all, so I tried to put it out of my mind as much as was possible.

Regardless it still niggled at me. I felt less safe with a sabre in my hand than I was used to. Truth told, what I really needed was an opponent to train with. Someone with whom I could gauge how much I needed to compensate for my monocular view. Unfortunately, there was the rub. I was short of opponents to choose from, ones I felt I trust at any rate.

There were the locals of course, but I wouldn't trust them with a real blade in their hands. Most of the other Europeans about were, if not openly hostile, untrusting towards me. Given the circumstances of my arrival, I'm not sure I blamed them for that. I was after all a representative of the very powers they worked against, albeit an unwilling one. It would not have surprise me over much if one of them took it upon themselves to act with a degree of expediency, and relieve their masters of the headache of deciding what to do with me.

There were also the Russian airmen working on their Iron Tsar's, those dreadful Russian airships I mentioned earlier. They were, for the most part, an amiable crew, and for all that I'm an officer, I have always found the company of the ranks easier than that of my fellows. A legacy of my youth, and the knowledge that by rights I was never destined to rise I suspect.

A bastard of the empire may find a role in the service, but he would never amount to much unless he could buy a higher commission, as I mentioned, and in doing so, there would always be those who questioned how he found the money. Besides, even with my illicit earnings, I would have struggled to find the money all the same. A love of the good life had always my downfall, that and a lack of real ambition beyond the next girl and the next bottle, if I am being entirely honest.

The Russian crews played cards in little groups in their off hours. I had even joined in a hand or two. Poker with Russian rules for Rubles was an interesting distraction on an evening particularly when they got the vodka out.

The rules were easy enough to follow all the same once I got my head around the differences between the cards. I managed to buy myself a stake with Rupees and after a few nights careful fleecing I was even up a few.

I could have won more, but something told me that raking in too much would be a cause of friction I would rather avoid. Most had some English, but they were always yammering away in Russian unless they spoke to me directly. My company was welcome as long as I didn't win too much, and laughed at their jokes. Carefully making sure I crashed a few good hands rather than take the pot helped. I was playing for entertainment not profit in the end, besides where was I ever going to spend the rubles?

But for all their easy comradeship I would never trust any of them to spar with. I have found it unwise, for all my fondness for the company of the rank and file, to put myself in a position where they could skewer me with three foot of steel and claim it was an accident.

I've never met a ranker who could honestly say they have never thought of doing an officer in, if they had the chance.

Be they Russian, French, English or any other damn nationality I imagine, enlisted men are same everywhere. They know they are the poor buggers who would do the brunt of the dying if things came to a fight, and they know which shiny brass button monkeys would be ordering them into the mincer.

Can't say I blame them for their resentment at this state of affairs overmuch, but I was not about to hand them an opportunity to spear a sword through me.

As for the Russian officers... Well... Their Captain was a strutting peacock of a man named Putin, who was somewhat overly beloved of both the tassels on his uniform and the medals on his chest.

I'd met his type before all too many times, he had the kind of pomposity that gives pompous a bad name. Besides which, how he came to be captain left me more than a little wary of him. He had not, so I am told, gained his commission from the Russian Air Ministry. Russian though his crew may have been, they were no more part of the Tsars Navy than I myself was now was part of 'Old Unamused's' fleet.

From my poker buddies, I managed to glean a little about how the Steel Tsar had left the service of its namesake. 'Captain' Vlad had been busy picking his crew for some years. They were to a man, men who had been dissatisfied with their lot. Easy to find among aircrews if you're looking for them, even among the British crews, though, as a rule, ours tended to be mostly loyal men.

Russia, however, was not the Queen's Empire. For all that the Tsar had modernised his country after the failed attempted Leninist coup all those years ago, it still kept its workers low. Most of the airmen were conscripts from the Ukraine, no more true Russians than the Irish are from England. I gathered from our faltering conversations that Vladimir, a lowly gun officer at the time had been trusted, for reasons that astound me if I am honest, having met the man, with recruiting crewmen. So he had been filtering more disgruntled Ukrainians into the crew of the Dreadnought for a year or more. While planning from the first, no doubt, to exploit their flexible loyalties to the Russian crown.

On a long patrol down into the Afghan mountains, he had taken his opportunity, and led his men in a coupe of his own. Killing the senior officers and other members of the crew whose loyalty he had not bought, before hightailing it down into Tibet. How they ended up here in the employ of my erstwhile hosts I cannot imagine. In the end, they now claimed to be mercenaries, but there is another word for it. No matter what they chose to call themselves, the crew of the Steel Tsar were now pirates.

Not that they were the first aircrew to turn pirate. It happened even with the Queen's ships once in a while. Though R.A.N. took an extremist view when it came to retaliation, and I'd not heard of it happening in years. With Russian crews, it was somewhat more common. Perhaps that was because they had more places to run. The Russian frontier was as good as endless. Siberia alone could swallow a fleet of ships with little risk of any ever being hunted down.

What Putin had offered his men to raise him to Captain I don't know. Though they all had more than enough Rubles on them, enough that they did not care about losing a few to me at any rate.

Money always buys the truest loyalties I have found over the years.

Of Vladimir himself, I'd seen little of him in several days, and all of that from a distance. He seemed very pleased with himself all the same. Enjoying his new reign as Captain of the beast that was the Russian ship. A little investigation over some passable vodka with an airman who spoke better English than most, revealed that Vladimir was actually only a second class gunnery officer in the Russian navy originally. So as a former first-class gunnery office in the RAN I guessed I outranked him. A snippet I'd kept to myself until such a time came as I could make use of it.

All the same, as a sparring partner, crossing swords with a traitorous opportunist like Vlad Putin left me cold, and the same went for any of his handpicked 'officers'. Men who I wouldn't trust to hold my vodka for me while I took a leak…

There were others around of course. Though I think I have digressed enough for now, so just assume there was no one with whom I would choose to cross swords. Even in a training yard. So solo sabre drills it was… With my silent audience watching on, cross-legged and eating rice from a bowl. His expression, as changeless as the mountains.

As the days went by, I grew listless. Bad vodka, card schools, and a lot of sitting around doing nothing, while nothing is exactly what anyone told you about your ultimate fate, is not much of a way to pass your days. It runs towards the dull, but the circumstances that brought me to that blasted little valley gave me little choice but to accept my lot.

I am not a man overly fond of accepting his lot. So the daily exercise routine helped me vent my frustrations a little. After a week or so I could feel the old reactions sharpening, the heavy training blade felt lighter in my hand, I had to push myself more to lose my breath and feel the burn of tired limbs. I felt stronger, sharper, and more like my old self after the recent trials the world had put me through.

A certain flamboyance in my training came with this, I will admit, which drew an even harder stare from my watcher. Not that I cared about his opinion, or anyone else's.

Actually, I tell a lie, there was at the monastery one who's good opinion I had some little care for. If I were to have an audience, I'd have preferred it to be a certain young lady of my acquaintance. The granddaughter of the leader of the strange band of Europeans I'd found myself surrounded by. Indeed I would have been delighted to impress her with my swordplay. Just as ultimately I hoped to impress her with another weapon of mine…

Sadly I suspected she was already less than impressed with me, given that our most recent meeting had occurred under unfortunate circumstances.

Circumstances which combined with a great deal of the local gut rot, a liquor they called Raki which ably doubled as paint stripper and bleach, led to me rather ungallantly vomiting all over her highly polished boots.

In my defence, I believed at the time I was being at-tacked by pirates and the airship on which I was serving as first officer had been taken by murderous cutthroats. So getting outrageously drunk and hiding in the aft compartments seemed wise at the time. I was, as stated, very drunk. Though in my defence I was also entirely correct about those attacking my ship…

That had been several weeks earlier, and I had seen neither hide nor hair of Miss Saffron Wells since then, and rather too much of the madman who professed, despite the obvious problems of his age relative to her own, to be her grandfather; Herbert. A man clearly only a decade or two her senior.

But I digress once more. Suffice to say Herbert Wells was running the whole shindig in the mountains, and he was the reason the British government had sent me to bloody India in the first place. Or at least, a shad-owy clandestine part of the government whose existence was not common knowledge, even amongst those who served in the government. It was the part that actually did things, whilst the rest of the govern-ment fooled itself into believing it was in charge.

Considering my options had been somewhat limited at the time of my commission, I should probably be thankful he was causing the Ministry so much concern. That I failed to feel overly thankful probably says something about me, but no one's motivations pass the muster of close investigation. I have found over the years, I am far from alone in that failing.

It must have been the second week or so of my new training regime when it happened. I walked up to the quadrant, just as the monks were bowing to each other and their teacher at the end of the morning session. I paused, with what could have been considered respect had it not been pinged with impatience, at the side of the square while they did this. I was in an irritable mood, my luck at the tables the night before had been foul.

I nodded with something below the bare minimum of respect to their trainer, monk in black, the one who always watched me. In my defence, I was not really aware of the insult I did him by doing this.

As I stepped into the square, loosening my sword arm a little and rocking my head from side to side to work out any kinks, I came up short when I spotted a beautifully scabbarded sabre laying in the centre of the square.

A small wooden frame was holding it up from the dusty clay. Had it sat on a table I would have called it displayed. Where it sat before me the word, presented, seemed the more obvious conclusion. I found myself wondering for a moment of self-justification, at the intricacies of the oriental mind. I was not sure what I had done to deserve such a gift, but that it was a gift to me was obvious in my avarice.

It was possibly the finest blade I've ever seen. Certainly the finest I've ever handled. I took its weight as I picked it up, it was heavier than I expected but not unduly so. I slid the blade out a quarter. The silvered steel was without blemish, polished with oil to the finest degree. Engraved swirling intertwining patterns followed the sweep of the blade. Unlike the blunted training sword I had been swinging about for days, this would be perfectly balanced. I could tell that just by looking.

Its hilt basket was crafted of interwoven gold wire that formed the imperial crest. The pommel stone was, an actual stone, a piece of granite carved into the noble head of a British lion.

This was an officer's blade, a senior officer's blade at that. A general or an admiral's blade. The kind of sword that got presented to those of great service by 'Old Iron Knickers' herself.

It was as much a piece of art as a weapon, its value was beyond my ability to calculate. It was certainly worth more than any blade I could ever have expected to hold in my hands.

I slipped the blade back into the scabbard without drawing it completely. Feeling the smooth sweep of the blade as I did so. It did not so much slide into its scabbard as glide. The craftsmanship of the scabbard as fine as that of the blade itself.

Then I slid it open once more, whilst I considered it next to my own blunted training blade of blackened steel.

I know what you're probably thinking.

I was probably thinking it myself on some level.

But avarice has a way of leading you down the garden path in such a way as you circumvent common sense entirely.

Well, it has for me anyway.

I threw my old blade aside and drew the sabre fully, letting the finely decorated scabbard fall to the ground as well. Discarding the scabbard with a degree of ignorant disdain, despite its outstanding craftsmanship, in my haste to feel the weight of the blade.

The balance was even more perfect than I'd first thought. I found myself taking a couple of practice sweeps, letting it glide through the air. For all its weigh it felt remarkably light in my hand compared to any other blade I had ever held like a true extension of my arm, even with this first hefting, it felt as much a part of me as my own flesh.

I did some figure eights, followed by gentle foe-ripostes. The movements felt so smooth in my hand. I could 'feel' the air as it sliced through. Parting before it as if cut by the blade itself.

I consider myself a fair swordsman as I have said, but with this blade, I knew I could best a master. I could best anyone, it was made for me, I now knew this, felt this, deep in my soul. No one could stand before me blade in hand and win. I knew this too, as sure as I knew my own name.

So, as you have no doubt determined, holding that blade, I was a tad prideful as well as bested by my avarice.

I was stocking up on the deadly sins, and what is it they say comes before the fall…

I started to follow the same drills I'd followed each day with the training blade. Sweep, sweep, step, step, riposte, block, step, thrust. Then turn through ninety degrees and repeat the pattern. Sweep, sweep, step, step, riposte, block, step, thrust.

It's a simple routine I had been taught at Rudgley School back when I was a cadet. A way to warm up the muscles, and build flexibility in the wrist.

Sweep, sweep, step, step, riposte, block, step, thrust.

Yet these movements had never felt so certain, so precise and graceful, as they did when I was holding that blade.

Sweep, sweep, step, step, riposte, block, step, thrust.

By the fourth repetition, I felt I had truly gotten the balance of the blade. So I started more complex forms. Imagining multiple opponents and fending them off.

I was at the end of a pattern ending in two thrusts when I spun back to another basic form. One which began an overhead sweep that came down as I rotated a half turn on my heel. But as the blade came down into the vacant air I knew was behind me…

The clang of steel on steel rang out across the court-yard, as a jarring impact shot through my arm.

My friend, the black-robed monk, stood before me. His face a blank mask, his sword was blocking my own.

His face was impassive. Inscrutable in that way the oriental face is often described by men who had never stared into the eyes of a small monk holding four feet of cold hard steel in their hands. Passionless, without anger, or any outward sign of emotion he just stared up at me.

He said something, not that I understood a word of his babble, but it sounded gentle, unthreatening, indeed had it not been for the sword he held I would have considered him at the moment to be the most un-aggressive of men.

We held form there for the length of a moment then gentle and unthreatening was in the wind.

He attacked with startling venom. Within the first couple of desperate blocks on my part, I was left with one unassailable thought. A thought that was an utter certainty.

The small black-robed master was attacking with the expressed aim of killing me where I stood.

CHAPTER THE THIRD

Falstaff's Wisdom

As you have noted, I have a scar on my cheek. This one, below my left eye. It's an inch long and on occasion somewhat livid if I have been in the sun. This then, is how I acquired said scar.

Now I could tell you in great and graphic detail of the sword fight between the black-robed master and me on that day. How I fought with skill and panache. The flaring of the mountain sun off our blades. The sound of clashing steel echoing through the tranquillity of the valley.

I could tell you how, as we fought back and forth across the square, a crowd gathered to perceive this spectacle. His pupils watching as their master struggled to find a form which could get past my dualist guard. Russian air-shipmen hawking loud bets upon the outcome of this clash of east and west. Cheering on each block and parry. Gasping at each riposte, each subtle faint and rally.

I could say, and with no small pleasure if it were true, how the delightful Saffron Wells came to watch this battle of British tenacity and grit, pitted against oriental perfidy and guile. I could tell you how she swooned despite herself when my footing slipped momentarily.

I could tell you how she breathed out in sharp relief when I caught myself and rallied once more. Caught up in the drama unfolding before her, as I fought with honour and tenacity she saw me anew, and with this fresh vision saw my worth at last...

I could tell you how this was the finest of duals. That in truth two masters battled across the square for hours that day. While the noon sun slowly descended until the cool of the evening set in... Until the day itself did seem to hold its breath in expectation before the sun would finally consent to drop below the line of the horizon.

I could tell you all this and more, a blow by blow account, which if written in a memoir would continue for several pages. Of how I bravely fought against him and won both the dual and his respect. Till he bent his knee to me and acknowledged me his master.

I, Hannibal Smyth, the finest of blades.

Paramore of the steeled edge.

Winning not just the fight, but the master's respect and the hearts of all those who watched...

I could tell you all this...

But I suspect you know I would be lying.

What actually happened then was this…

He attacked, and I defended as best I could against the fury of his blows. I turned his blade twice, more by luck than judgment. Then he swiftly disarmed me sending the sword I had so briefly possessed into the clay at our feet. Then with precision like that of a surgeon, he flashed the tip of his blade across my cheek where this scar now lays.

Which, I may add, stung like hell.

I tried to stem the bleeding with my hand, and felt the blood rushing through my fingers, while he just stood back and stared up at me. Once more a picture of tranquil repose. Dismissively he wiped my blood from his blade with a piece of silk, then slipped the sword back into the wooden scabbard tied to his waist, in one slow, graceful movement.

Then, without so much as a bow or an acknowledgement of any kind, he simply turned and walked away, which even an ill-educated fool such as I knew for the darkest of insults…

It was something of a humbling experience.

Not to mention a bitter tasting, utterly enraging experience.

I almost grabbed the fallen sword that lay no more than two strides from me.

Grabbed it and had at him while he walked away.

Almost…

Shakespeare tells us Falstaff's imparted some notable wisdom to Henry. To which I would add my own. Discretion may be the better part of valour, but cowardice is the better part of discretion. Fear may make fools of us all, but I knew at that moment with utter certainty that should I pick up that blade I would not have lived to tell this tale.

So tempted though I was so pick up that blade once more, it was only ever almost…

Later, though not so much later the bleeding had been fully stemmed, and nowhere near later enough that pride had returned, while I sat nursing a bottle of vodka I had snaffled from a Russian crewman, it was explained to me that I had insulted the black-robed monk.

This came as no great shock to be fair, given this explanation came to me after he had so acutely demonstrated his displeasure.

What I really wanted to know, however, was why.

The man who imparted this news to me was a monk himself. One of the black-robes less able students. An odd little fellow who called himself Go Chi. He had a nervous look in his eyes when he spoke. I realised, with surprising insight on my part, all things considered, that this was because he should not have been by talking to me at all. I had no doubt that in so doing, he was risking the master's displeasure himself. To this day I'm not sure why he did so.

"One not enter the training square without asking for the master's allowance." He explained in his faltering version of the mother tongue, which, it must be said, was far better than my Hindi or Nepalese or whatever barbarous language the locals spoke at the monastery.

There was an earnest intensity to the little man, in other circumstances I would have probably liked him. Smiling helpfully he continued, "One must bow like this," and performed a perfect genuflection to me so I understood, "And then one must ask to train. It is important that one must show humility."

"Bloody humility, are you mad," I replied, though snapped would be closer to the truth of it.

I was not in the mood to go showing humility to anyone, least of all that little black-robed monk.

I believe I called him something distasteful. Which strictly speaking should have been beneath me.

I am not one as a rule to belittle the native peoples like some of my fellow Imperials. Not as a rule at any rate. The idea that the British are superior in some way to other races, in particular, the races within the Empire, I find utterly ridiculous.

In part, this is due to the low station of my own birth. Being born in the slums of London was after all not much different from the slums of Dehli or Cairo or any of the other mighty cities of the empire. Where I grew up, you lived on the scraps and leavings of the rich either way, regardless of the colour of your skin.

The poor are their own race and all as one in my eyes. Though there are many who grew up around me, who would disagree, I have no doubt.

The belief in the superiority of the British runs deep, even to the darkest, lowest, and most flea-bitten holes in London. The superiority of those born upon the sceptered isle is considered a given by many. It's a point of pride for them. They believe, despite the filth, they stumble through each day, that to be British is to be better than any other race. Be you a Lord in a high castle or a shit skiver on the banks of the Thames.

It's a bloody ridiculous notion I know.

I think perhaps it is simply that I escaped such an existence to join the ranks of those above the station of my birth that gave me the ability to see the lie of

British superiority. That the only thing we are better at than other nations, is building machines of destruction and stealing from those with fewer guns. We are not the chosen of God, nor was Jerusalem built on an English cricket pitch. There is nothing better about standing in the sewer, just because it is a British sewer. The same shit piles up around your ankles…

We British for all our pomp and imperially instilled pride, are no more than the biggest bullies in the playground.

But all the same, better to be within the lie than outside it, and sometimes, despite myself, I slip back to the East End slum mentality.

So as I was saying…

"Bloody slant eye bastard has scarred me for life, and you think I should bow and scrape to him. I am a Bloody Englishman you god damned arse. One of the superior race. The race of kings, I'm one of Victoria's benighted children. Our empire never sees bloody sunset, I am British god damn you, and we bow to no bastard goat fucker in the arse end of the fucking world…"

Tact was not one of my stronger points right then.

Go Chi bowed to me, smiling despite my anger and showing the kind of humility that was utterly beyond me at that moment. Then he left me to my raging. With hindsight, I should perhaps have listened.

If I had returned to the quadrant and bowed before the black robe, I might have impressed him with my own humility.

Had I served at his feet I may have won his respect over time?

I may have learnt the secrets of eastern meditation, of the oriental fighting arts, of chi and woe shan. The way of the furious tiger, wise badger, and the artful crane.

In time, my humiliation forgotten, my lessons learned, I would no doubt become his finest student. Perhaps in time even finally surpassing the master?

Then, having learned all the wisdom he could teach me, gained his respect and found my inner chi... I could have left a damn great scar on his cheek.

It is probably what you expected to happen next. The moving lantern shows, and a raft of below-par fiction have no doubt prepared your expectations. It is, after all, an age-old story. The arrogant pupil humbled by the master learns a lesson in humility and respect...

I apologise if this is the case, for letting you down.

Though no doubt if that had happened, I would have ended up respecting the master and all the rage I felt towards him would have been dissipated just before he was killed by one, who would become my arch enemy. Then I would spend the latter half of the story tracking down his killer, facing many trials and tribulations aplenty before exacting revenge in my master's name.

You see I have read Penny Dreadful Kung Fu novels too...

Two hundred feet down...

Hannibal's tale trailed off, as he drank the last of the pint in front of him before standing and straightening his jacket.

He smiled a self-effacing kind of smile and said. "That is, however, not what happened next. What did, well that is tale for another time. Suffice to say I did not learn much humility and I did not go on to study with the master. That is though the story of how I got this scar on my cheek, since you asked."

Richard finished his own beer and stood up himself, holding out his hand to the strange airman. "It was...

It's been a pleasure…" he replied, surprising himself by realising he spoke the truth.

Whatever else Hannibal's story had been, it had brought a smile to his face, though he suspected there were as many lies bound up within in it as there were truths in the tale.

"But anyway I should get off old boy. I need to get back to… back to… Hum, for the life of me I not sure where I need to get back to, I was definitely doing something important before I got here… I am sure it will come back to me…"

For a moment the man looked confused, an expression Richard knew only too well. He had seen it before when someone in the Passing Place realised it is time to leave. That moment of slight bewilderment, when they could not quite remember where they were, or how they actually got there in the first place. It took some worse than others, and Hannibal seemed to have a particularly bad case of it.

Most people had at least been looking for the bar, or a bar at any rate, which was why they passed through the doors in the first place. On occasion, however, it was not quite so simple… Sometimes people were pulled in, metaphorically at least, and others just found themselves there for reasons that would never be explained to them. Richard occasionally wondered if at some point he would find himself in that self-same bemused state. If he was in fact, just passing through and would forget all this when he left? Was his just an extended visit, while the bar needed someone to tickle the ivories for a while?

Whatever the truth of it, when such thoughts occurred to him he pushed them aside. The longer he stayed in Esqwith's strange abode, the less he considered wanted to think about the answers to those questions. It was, in a word, becoming home.

A strange beguiling and utterly impossible home though it may be.

Richard found his gaze seeking out Sonny Burbank, the Passing Place's resident doorman. The big man was, to Richards's lack of surprise, already looking in the direction of the pair of Englishmen and smiling his knowing smile back at the piano player.

"Falling, was I falling…?" Hannibal was muttering, as Richard started gently guiding him towards the exit.

"I'm sure it will be fine…" Richard told him with empty certainty.

Hannibal frowned and took the deep breath of the worried, then suddenly seemed to perk back up. "Oh no doubt, till next time then old chap. Was nice to meet you, toodle pip as it were." The Airman said with a smile that suggested the last was a deliberate bit of self-effacement.

"You too Hannibal, mind how you go…" The piano player replied as they reached the doorway, and Sonny stepped to one side to let the departing patron pass.

With that, Hannibal flashed up a self-mocking salute to both Sonny and Richard and stepped through the door into…

"Nothing…" Richard said.

He and Sonny were relaxing at the bar an hour or two after closing.

The lights were dim, the place was quiet as the rest of the staff had wandered off to bed, or wherever they went on an evening, so the pair were enjoying a brandy together and the silence, both of rare quality.

Mostly, Richard had been watching Sonny gently swirling brandy around the bowl of his glass, as a long moment had dragged out between them. Until the thought which had been bugging him for hours found voice.

"Nothing… He stepped into nothing." He said again, catching Sonny's eye as he did so. "Hannibal, the British guy in the uniform I was talking to earlier. He stepped out into nothing, just empty space…"

The Brandy glass stopped swirling as Sonny Burbank returned the piano players gaze, and for a moment the silence held between them once more. Then the big man smiled, a smile which said it was going to be one of 'those' conversations, a smile of resignation to the inevitable, though Richard had come to suspect that Sonny enjoyed 'those' conversations, with more than a little merry devilment. With a gentle shake of his head, the doorman's smile got wider.

"Not nothing, he stepped out into the air. Which is definitely something. Nothing, now that's something else entirely, you've been out to Morn's garden, you've seen what nothing is…" The Doorman said and commenced swirling his brandy once more.

Then, for a fleeting moment, Richard saw something cross Sonny's expression. A note of concern, a momentary flicker of disquiet. Richard felt it as well, he always did if he was drawn to consider what lay beyond the borders of Morn's garden. That nothing which Sonny spoke of, was the endless nothing of the void, the space between universes, it would disquiet anyone… And yet… It was not the emptiness, that endless absence of anything, which caused Richard to feel uneasy. It was what that endless void might contain that scared him. That feeling which would creep upon you when you beheld it. The feeling that out there in all that nothing, there was something. Something sinister, something wrong, something watching you back, a hungry something, something with eyes that could eat into your soul.

Even thinking of it now, for a fleeting moment, Richard felt smaller, and cold, so very cold. Just knowing it was there, in the void, waiting, watching, reaching towards them…

Something the colour of an open wound…

Something…

"Two hundred feet…" Sonny said suddenly. Snapping the thought out of Richard's mind. It was the unusually sharp tone of voice the Doorman used which did it. So uncharacteristic of the big man. Bringing Richard back to the present. The strange feeling of being observed, which had overtaken him, fled from his consciousness.

"What?" Richard asked, realising his attention had drifted, though for the life of him he couldn't remember what it was he had been thinking about a moment ago. '*Must be getting tired,*' he explained to himself, and looked up from his own glass to see Sonny's smile looking back at him.

"Two hundred feet…" Sonny repeated, more softly now he had Richards's attention, his delicate southern Carolina tones soothing somehow, and the piano player forgot that he had forgotten what he was thinking.

"More or less anyway, two hundred feet above what, at a guess was the middle of the Indian Ocean. That was what Harry stepped out into. So not nothing, thin air perhaps, but defiantly not nothing."

"What?" Richard asked, then, aware he was repeating himself he added. "And? We're okay with this? I mean, seriously?"

Sonny chuckled slightly, "Oh I have no doubt he'll survive, it's what he's best at after all."

"Falling two hundred feet into the Indian Ocean is what he's best at? That's an odd talent." Richard said, sounding as incredulous as he felt.

"No, not that… Well I mean, yes, in actuality it is exactly the kind of thing he is good at… But what I meant was surviving. Harry Smith is one of the universe's natural survivors, the old girl has a habit of seeing him right, one way or another. Though I suspect Harry doesn't see it that way…" the doorman said, a lilt of humour to his voice once more, that slightly mocking warm humour with which he seemed to approach everything in life.

Richard smiled at his friend. Sonny had a way of seeing the humour in most everything. It was hard not to see it too, even when he was being his normal overly cryptic self. Then a thought occurred to the Englishman.

"Hang on 'Harry' you're the second person to call him Harry, yet he said his name was Hannibal…" Richard said, not even realising as he did so, that he was counting the cat as a person. Though if he had stopped to think about it, he almost certainly would have done so anyway.

The Doorman shrugged and smiled once more. Imparting with this ambivalence that it did not really matter what the guy had called himself.

Richard refilled his brandy and offered the bottle to the Doorman who accepted it with a sigh, half filled his glass then sat back and began swirling the brandy around it in an absentminded way before he spoke again.

"Harry, or Hannibal if you prefer, is, well just one of those who turns up at our door now and again. His names not always the same, Harry Smith, Hannibal Smyth, Henry Smiting's, whatever he is going by at the time. It's normally close enough, one way or another. The name that is. And well, he probably doesn't even remember being here before, or like as not, remember being here after he leaves. Or maybe he does, who knows. Let's just say he, or some version of him, has from time to time, a habit of dropping in …" Sonny said and could not keep a little laughter from his voice at the last.

He fought it bravely for a few moments after he had finished speaking but then started to laugh with that deep hearty laugh of his at a joke Richard was not entirely sure he got at first…

And then he did, as the penny dropped.

"When you say dropping in, you mean he literally…" he started to ask before Sonny's infectious laughter caught hold of him too, as Sonny nodded back at him, affirming the question Richard had not quite asked…

It took a few moments for the two of them to get control of themselves, for all that after the laughter started to die out Richard was not wholly sure why it was so funny. Though Sonny had a way about him that made you see the humour in the oddest situations.

After catching his breath for another moment, Sonny continued. "Well yes, this time at any rate, quite literally. From what I gathered when he landed on the doorstep after he'd left an airship about a couple of hundred foot above us earlier. As I told you, the universe has a habit of taking care of him. I think it arranged for us to catch him on the way down."

"Oh come on, you can't be serious, the universe doesn't arrange things, the universe is not… it doesn't… it's just the universe."

Sonny shrugged.

It was that same old '*But what do I know, I'm just the Doorman*' Shrug Richard had gotten so used to since taking up residence in the Passing Place. Then the doorman took a drink of his brandy and shrugged once more…

"Well maybe that's true, maybe the universe just is and its something in the universe rather than the universe itself taking care of old Harry out there. Maybe it's just this place, I wouldn't put it past her. Catching him when he falls and nudging things along that way. You know how she likes a good story…"

"What I do know is this, every once in a while old Harry turns up, has a couple of beers, tells a tale that may just be true, or at least some version of a truth, his version at least. Then off he goes again, not quite on exactly the same trajectory as when he arrived. Maybe Harry is just very lucky that way, or maybe not? You've read Moorcock right?"

Richard nodded, with the slightest suspicion of where the conversation was going. Sonny had a thing about Michael Moorcock novels, Richard had never quite worked out why. Though he had read them himself in his late teens, and if you took them as being something more than mere fiction, they explained a lot about the Passing place. But that was an illogical leap too far even for Richard. He had found himself accepting a lot of things on faith of late, but something were just too hard to fathom. But regardless of the piano players incredulity Sonny continued with his analogy…

"Well, that whole multiverse, eternal champion thing, different incarnations of the same hero cropping up time and time again across all the different worlds, the different versions of the universe… Well Harrys like that, well, sort of at any rate."

Richard felt his credulity being stretched a little thin and said "He didn't seem much of a hero, he was more, well you know…" which started Sonny laughing once more.

"Well yer, that's true, but the way I see it, if there is some kind of eternal champion in the multiverse, then it stands to reason that you need someone like Harry Smith to balance the books a little. So I reckon he is a sort of eternal bumbling buffoon, cursed, if you will, to get the wrong end of the stick throughout all eternity, make a mess of everything, and yet somehow manage to stumble through regardless. An eternal everyman as it were."

Richard thought about this for a moment. Despite the ridiculousness of the idea, it made a strange kind of sense. Within its own argument at any rate. What was more, if there was a grain of truth to it, then it was somehow vaguely reassuring, he felt, that the universe could work that way. At the same time, he felt it was mildly terrifying to think that it did. Though he could not explain exactly why he thought that either…

"So hang on, if I'm buying any of this, and I am not saying I do." Richard said after a while, "Then what exactly did we change. He was falling into the ocean when he arrived, started falling into the ocean again when he left. So nothing's changed he is still going to land in the middle of the Indian Ocean…"

Sonny nodded and shrugged once more, and then sipped down the last of his brandy, before getting to his feet and pulling his tuxedo coat back on. Clearly having decided, with a certain degree of convenience given the way the conversation was going, it was time for him to head to his bed. Though that was Sonny all over, cryptic explanations which made sense to a degree, yet left so many more unanswered questions, closely followed by an exit which left Richard more confused than he was before.

That said, Richard realised suddenly how tired he now felt. His glass now empty, he decided it was time to head up to bed himself. So he gave his friend a mock salute and started towards the staircase that led to his room, but he did not get far before Sonny raised his hand to stop him for a moment.

"You're right, he still landed in the middle of the Indian Ocean." The Doorman said a mischievous grin crossing his lips… "But, and I think this is the important bit, he landed in the waters of the Indian Ocean, as opposed to landing bang smack on top of Monsieur Verne's submarine…"

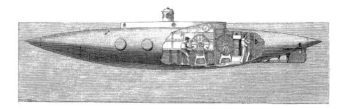

An End...

For now...

Author's notes

Relativity of Location

Esqwith's Passing Place is a Piano Bar and Grill, just this side, or perhaps just the other side, of reality. It is a place where people tell stories, some funny, some dark, some heart-wrenching. It is also a place with a story of it's own. It's never quite the same any time you visit it. Though there are constants if you know where to look, which also makes it a convenient place for characters from one story to bump into characters from another.

Richard, Sonny, The Cat and the rest of the inhabitance of Esqwith's have a long self-contained tale of their own which is told in my Novel "Passing Place".

The Passing Place parts of this novelette take place in between a couple of chapters of 'Passing Place'.

While they have no real influence on events in that novel, those readers who may wish to know exactly when this tale falls within it. It's after the Inuit's tale of tears and before Richard visits the forest in the cellar. If that seems vague, even to those who have read the novel, that's because it's meant to be…

Hannibal Smyth, otherwise known as Harry Smith, or as Sonny would have you believe The Eternal Bumbling Buffoon… Recants a longer episodes from his life in 'The Hannibal Smyth Misadventures' series of novels starting with 'A Spider In The Eye' and continuing in 'From Russia With Tassels' and the fore coming 'A Squid On The Shoulder' He lives in a world where the British Empire never saw its sunset, and Good old Queen Vic is soon to celebrate her Bi-centennial on the throne. How exactly Old Iron Knickers is still on the throne? Is she as unamused as ever? What indeed has gone wrong with the history of the 20th century? And How Hannibal finds himself caught up in events due to the machinations of the Ministry? All these are questions that you'll have to read the novels to find answers to.

Hannibal also appears in the 'Harvey Duckman presents' anthologies, telling shorter tales of his Misadventures.

The events he imparts in this novelette take place somewhere in the midst of that tale, after he arrives in Nepal on the trail of the architect of several unfortunate events that have befallen, well you'll have to wait and see.

As to how he ends up falling into the Indian Ocean and narrowly missing Jules Verne's Submarine… that is another tale…

Extra Bits

Esqwith's Passing Place is a Piano Bar and Grill just this side, or perhaps on the other side, of reality. It is a place where people tell stories, some funny, some dark, some heart-wrenching. Stop me if you have heard that before...

When writing Passing Place, I wrote a lot of stories which for one reason or another never made it to the final Novel. Usually just because they did not quite fit with the overall tale, or a better story came together for the part of the novel they were originally destined to inhabit. Some are destined to be a part of 'Something

Red,' the sequel to 'Passing Place' which is slowly coming together. Others have gone off and become the seeds for Novels of their own, and are sat on my hard drive waiting for me to write them. But the tales still exist that fall somewhere between the two in a strange little void. It doesn't make them lesser tales. Just the ones that got told one night in Esqwith's, but I have never related beyond that. This is one such tale, included here for no reason other than the core idea appeals to me. It is a little disjointed, as an idea, it's not fully formed and I may one day make more of it. It is also one of the nasty ones so, then let's just say…

The Devil Made Me Do It

"A good cop never reads his old case files" that's what Hannagan had told him on his first day as a detective. But then Hannagan was that kind of cop.

Hannagan would not read old case files because they might throw up too many questions. You nailed someone for a crime, you made it stick, and then you let the courts bang them away forever with any luck. There was no point reading old case files after that.

According then to Hannagan's oft imparted wisdom… Old files were full of the questions you never answered, like why the man seen running away from the scene of the crime was five foot three with blonde hair, but the collar was a six-foot black guy who was seen in the area a few days afterwards.

Maybe all the case file was, in the end, was a wad of circumstantial evidence that added up to a case. Maybe that wasn't an airtight case, but it was at least one that would hold air long enough to get a conviction. And if the collar were a known bad guy, even if he did not do the crime in question, he would have done something so what then did it matter? One more low life off the streets.

No sense reading the old case file after the event. Such things were buried in the recesses of lost filing cabinets for a reason. Just move on to the next case, and find a guy who fits it.

That was Hannagan's wisdom for you, as straightforward as it gets in some ways.

Rick Richards was not a good cop, at least, not in the way Hannagan described a good cop. Richards cared more about getting the right guy than he did getting a conviction. Richards wanted scum off the street alright, but he wanted the right scum off the right streets for the things they had actually done, not just what you could make stick to them.

So Rick read his old case files once in a while and worried. *'Did I get the right guys?'*

As he got older, and more grizzled than even the veteran Hannagan had been back in the day, he read them all the more. He read them late at night when insomnia bit hard at his mind. He read them and drank whiskey by the finger. One finger a night,. Two on a bad one, three if he started to find something in an old file that niggled at him…

Tonight he was on his fourth finger, it was three am and sleep eluded him as he read yet another old case file, the St. Quentin murders.

All the evidence pointed to Jacobson. All the evidence added up. Yet there was that one bit right at the end, the same bit there always was right at the end, because they all seemed to say it. All the really bad ones, and it niggled at Rick, an itch at the back of his mind, more so than usual this night.

Jacobson was going to the chair in the morning. Old Sparkie himself. Rightly, as far as Rick was concerned, the bad guy went to the chair, at least if he was guilty. But there was the nub of it…

Richards had no problem with the death penalty, some crimes, well they deserved the ultimate sanction, but you had to be sure. Rick had to be sure. And not *'the jury convicted him unanimously'* sure. That was an easy sure.

He had to be sure in himself, sure he covered everything, certain that he had the right guy. Or how do you live with yourself when you've sent a guy to the chair…

So old case file it was, If only to determine once again that Jacobson did it and knew what he did when he swung that hammer…

Leastways, you did if you were the bad kind of cop. The kind of cop that read old case files at three in the morning on your fourth finger of whisky. The kind of Cop Richards was.

The kind of cop who worried about that bit at the end, that bit which was always there, the bit they all said, all claimed, what if that was true, what if 'he' really did make them do it. You know the line, the words they say, and you've all heard them say them.

"The devil made me do it."

If Rick had a dollar for every time… Well, he would be drinking better scotch for a start.

They always seemed to say it, "The devil made me

do it." And Rick, being the cop he was, always heard them say it. Without fail, without exception, when it came down to the last, "The devil made me do it."

It seemed to Rick that maybe there was a price to be paid, a debt to call in, and he had spent his life calling people in on debts like that. Locking them up and throwing away the key, one way or another, be it a jail cell or a bullet from his gun, he took them all, in the end.

And every time, every one of them, they all said the same thing, "The devil made me do it…"

At 3 am, insomnia biting, on his fourth finger of whisky, he got to thinking, what if…

What if 'he' did…

Rick knew the rules, he knew there were some laws, the laws of an authority beyond human justice, but if the devil did make them do it, it was the devil who should be brought to pay for the crimes. Someone had to bring him in, someone had to go down to hell, rain in the bastard and hold him to account.

Rick was raised a Catholic, and there was only one sure way he knew to go down there, to go have a reckoning with the one who made them all do it. One sin for which there was no absolution because you could not ask for absolution after the fact, not for that one.

Anything else you did you could seek forgiveness for, you could take your last rites and confess your sins before God. Absolution would be granted, no harm no foul...

Except for that one.

That one was a one-way ticket, sure as you like.

So on a spring night, after one too many whiskeys, Rick did the one thing he knew for sure would take him to his quarry,

"The devil made me do it." That's what they always say...

"Well now, the devils going to pay..." Rick Richards whispered to himself as he turned his service 38 so the barrel pointed back at him, and with the grimmest determination, he pulled the trigger ....

Extra Bits2

One Man's Utopia is another man's dystopia. This is a sad fact of the human condition. Henry Rawls once proposed that the biggest problem with democracy was people. Because people are, when it comes down to it, people.

People may say they want equality, a society build on freedom, liberty and fairness for all. But what they actually mean is they want equality, a society build on freedom, liberty and fairness for themselves on their terms, and everyone else to agree to live by their terms.

So when it comes to voting, they vote purely on their preference, without giving a damn about anyone else's. Rawls said this was a problem. You don't have to look far in modern politics to see he's not entirely wrong.

The question is how exactly do you get around that problem, and if you did, how could you be sure you really had…

After all, one man's utopia is just …

The Ballot

Every fourth year, on the anniversary of my birth, I perform my public duty and visit a Rawls booth. There is no law which states I must, no obligation on any of us to do so. Yet we each do so at some point in our lives. Above each booth is a legend.

'A choice which is not made freely is no choice at all'.

So it should be, so it is, yet I know of no one who does not make that choice. The one we all make and have done since the neo-reformation. The choice to enter the booths, the choice to exercise our political will.

I have been told that once visiting a booth was compulsory. An act of law, forced upon us by the state, so those who doubted Rawls wisdom could see they were in error. The histories tell us from amongst the unenlightened there were outcries and demonstrations. Something called 'the army' had to be used to make people join the first lines at the booths.

These though are enlightened days, the wisdom of Rawls has been seen by all. Now it is a duty, a compulsion, even a need perhaps, which we all feel. A duty to each other, for, after all, we live in the grace the booths have granted us.

A statue of Professor Cymene stands alongside a statue of the long-dead Rawls in the public park which was once called Parliament Square. Their marble visages have about them a look of serenity, a reflection of the legacy granted us by their labours. I have always thought it is a shame that Rawls never saw his dreams put into practice.

The booths are named for that long-dead social scientist. In that bygone era of strife, he lived through, he proposed an experiment of the mind. A thought experiment, for the technology to achieve his aim would never come to pass, he was sure. It was nothing more than a hypothetical set of circumstances, constructed to put forward a political idea. In his time he was respected, but he never gained the fame of others of his ilk.

His ideas seemed too abstract, too simplistic, lacking the innate Germanic fury of Marx, or progressive French charm of Rousseau. Rawls ideas were considered little more than worthy, but the impossibility of putting his experiment into practice consigning him as a footnote in the annals of academia.

That was until Cymene invented the booths, and then Rawls fame eclipsed all the others.

For all this, I find entering a booth hateful. For all my intellect lets me understand its reason for existing. For all, I know it is a fleeting state I will enter. For all, I understand what it is that it does to me. Going through the process makes my skin crawl.

I was taught, as we all were as children, about the booths in the simplistic terms they use for the young. They tell us it unburdens our psyche, so we may choose what is right. Then they show us as children, it was simpler then. Childhood naivety makes the process quick and easy. I think this is because while we are still growing into who we shall be, changing so rapidly, the process of the booth seems more natural to us.

As we grow older, and with it more assured of the self, they go into the details, give us a fuller understanding, some learn to fear the booths then, though only for a little while. Some say it feels more like losing something once you understand that there is something being lost. Rather than a putting aside of self, it feels like having something stripped away. A peeling of the self-image we construct around ourselves, that which tells us who we are. To be willing to subject those hollow egos, we have so lovingly built, to the machine, we have to understand the why as well as the how.

So we are taught to understand how things were without Rawls principals governing our lives. Each much accept the good that they do, so we will allow ourselves to be subjected to the machine. Only through understanding can we accept it. Without acceptance, we would fight against the process, struggle against the stripping away, which would make it so much harder upon us.

On entering the booth, I am immersed in total darkness. All light and sound from beyond the booth is extinguished. I am isolated from the world, placed apart for everything beyond. After the longest of moments, small pinpricks of lights start to flash in the air around me. A swelling of sound fills the air, surrounding me with discordant cords, too base to be called music. I become disorientated, confused, distance becomes imperceptible. The sounds echo around me but indistinct, there could be words buried within the sounds or music with harmonies and counterpoints, poetry or verse and credence or the cries of wounded animals and the sound of the wind blowing through abandoned halls. In these moments, I feel placed beyond, in a primal place, like a returning to the womb. These moments are without time, or progression, they are just a holding state, moments of preparation before the true process begins.

When the true process of the machine finally begins, I panic, as I always do. Fighting against it, despite knowing intellectually there is neither point nor need. Knowing this makes no difference. I still hate the feeling of their application. The primal id deep within me rebels against it, this slow surrender of self, this stripping away of identity. These little agonies of that self being pulled apart, each little part of me that is stripped away feels a wrenching of my personality, leaving small chasms in the whole. Some, those given to melodrama, have called it the stripping of the soul. I do not consign myself to such melodramas for all I understand their argument. But despite accepting it on a cerebral level, I fight it anyway, on the most basic of levels. Yet no matter how wildly I fight, I know it is required, this loss of self, for how else could I make true choices without the objectivity which only Cymene's machine can bring.

What the machine subtracts is the knowing of me, but only the knowing of me. After a few moments within its embrace I no longer know my position in the world, such unimportant matters as if I am a member of the rich or one of the poor. I lose the memory of my job, or if I even have one. My understanding of these concepts remains but I no longer know the status given to me in society by wealth. Am I a wage slave working forty grinning hours a week to pay the rent. Or perhaps, a high rolling investor in businesses with expense accounts and sharp suits? Do I live in a mansion or a council tenancy or perhaps, am I homeless? Scraping an existence, or living a life of privilege. I could be any of these things. How could I choose ethically, matters of taxation, or social welfare while thinking only of how it affects myself? In unknowing I am free to choose for the better for all.

The machine progresses, beginning to strip me back further to the core. I am fighting it less now, having lost something of self already, there is less urge to cling to what remains. Soon while I understand the genders, I no longer associate myself with male or female. While understanding all aspects of sexuality, I no longer know if I am straight or gay. I could be bisexual perhaps or asexual or anything else for that matter. I have all knowledge of these things and what it is to be them, but no longer the knowledge of my own sexuality, or how my own could bend my view on all others.

Concepts such as religion and faith I understand, but if I have faith myself, I no longer remember. This is not to say the machine strips belief from me, nothing so crude and debase as that. The beliefs I have remain, but are suppressed within me, put to one side for this short time. Instead, it places me in a frame of reference where I can accept all faiths and simultaneously none at the same time. Placing me in a state where I am intrinsically neutral to such concepts. If there is a god, how could he object to such a state of grace?

The machine has no mirrors or reflective surfaces, not that they would matter as it first dampens down, and then fully removes my perceptions of self. While an understanding of such concepts of race, of skin colour, of ethnicity, remain. I soon have no more idea of my own than I do of my gender. Soon after this I am lifted and held in a stream of null, weightless, and unbound by gravity. My senses undergoing deprivation within the machine; I float in a state of nullity. No influence from beyond can reach me and I have no will for them to do so.

More of my self is stripped back until the I in the machine, the I that I have become, no longer knows if I am able-bodied or disabled, if I am thin or fat, athletic or a couch potato. It takes all this from my awareness, while leaving the knowledge of these concepts whole. Other things of the I are taken. I understand the need of society to raise its children; I understand the concepts of parenthood. Why some chose it and others do not, but not if I am a parent or would chose to be. The machine takes from me all these things. Until while I understand concepts of everything, I know my own place in none of them. Here in this place, in this machine, I am a person, just a person, in as simple a form as can be. Not black or white, rich or poor, male or female, gay or straight, or any of the other endless combinations of definitions that separate us out from each other. I am just a person, a singular representative of humanities whole. A singular id, just one of the collective of us, and now, at last, I can vote.

The questions stream across the darkness before me. Projections or a non-reflective terminal screen, I know not. In this state, stripped to the core of my humanity, one of the us, I answer them. All these questions once the realm of Politian's, elected by proxy to run our lives. How should we be taxed? How should we live? Should there be tolerance of all? Should the sexes be equal? Should each have domain over their own body? Abortion? Contraception? Religious freedom? Freedom of expression? Rights? Healthcare? And a hundred more. All the questions summed up as 'What kind of society do we want to live in?' and I answer them in the state of the us. The state of the everyone.

The concept of the machine is simple. Within it we vote honestly and fairly, strip away of all the things which would once have made us vote according to our own selfishness and preconceptions. In the machine the only stake we hold is the one of the universal person, the "everyone" personified. Only then can we choose the society we truly wish to be in. This is Cymene's machine, this is Rawls principal in action, and this is how we achieved utopia. I vote, as we all vote.

Afterwards, I am returned from the universal us to the singular of me. I am all the things that define me once more. And can take my place again within the society of us. This is how we ended the tyranny of the individual. How we survived before the machine as a species is something beyond me.

There are those, those who remain beyond the machine, who would claim the me that entered the machine is changed when I leave it. The cynics who believe the machine programs us to accept this utopia. That it changes us in subtle ways, so that we accept the machine as a saviour of our society. That to do otherwise would be wrong, no matter how the laws it has created affect us as individuals. These voices of dissent are few and the peace we live in is a tribute to Rawls in that they are allowed a voice, allowed by the society of the us to cling to their old ways. They make speeches, write political blogs, call in to talk shows and decry the Rawls conspiracy. Such voices of dissent seldom last however. For in time they too must enter a booth to vote. It is their duty after all. How else could they exercise political will?

Afterwards, they always state publicly how wrong they were to distrust the machine.

And in the machine, we trust...

And Goblins

It has been a running joke that I would include one of my goblin stories in my next book since before publishing the Passing Place. Mainly, according to the joke, because then I can say:

'With added Goblins'

On the cover...

No, I don't know why that's funny either, perhaps you had to be there.

The there in question was a bar in Blackpool where a bunch of delightful geeks gather each year to play board-games, tell bad jokes, drink brown beer, and generally be a bit ridiculous.

We have been doing so for more years than I care to admit, and I suspect we'll be doing it for more years to come than I care to contemplate. But for those geeks (who are amongst the finest friends a man can have), and all the other geeks in the world who may appreciate this next bit of silliness.

This is the first of the somewhat infamous 'Goblin' stories from my original blog. It is silly, contrived and may have been inspired by a game played on table tops with small grey plastic that may or may not have been painted… I deny such a thing all the same… Except to say…

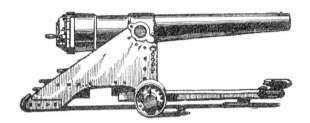

WARrrrrrrgggggg!!!!!!!

ReelBadBuga kicked the runt goblin out of his way, not with any great intent, just absent minded annoyance at having followed the little runt for two miles from the tribe's campsite.

He was a Big Boss he did not get summoned to the mountain. Runts don't summon a big boss. Runts don't send other runts with a summons for a Buga. This was the way of things, even if the mushroom eating runt in question were Mushmuncha the Shaman and touched by Glod.

The runt goblin flew towards the edge of the mountain track and over it, madly scrambling for purchase, with his hands flailing around. He grabbed a tree branch or managed to hold on at the last moment.

Luckily for him, ReelBadBuga had not bothered to go and look; he didn't even listen out for a satisfying scream followed by a small goblin sized squelch as it hit the bottom of the gorge. He was too focused on annoyance, and his temper was a thing of legend among the nineteen tribes of the Glod stone valley.

Rumour had it when ReelBadBugga stubbed a toe you could hear his roar of anger echo around the mountains from one end of the valley to the other for a week.

When one of Gurt Scarbutt's wolf riders used Reel's helmet for a chamber pot at a gathering three summers ago, he had taken the Buga's Boyz tribe to war. Driven by his fury the Buga's had ravaged their way through to the Scarbutts camps, decimating three other tribes who had the misfortune to be camped in the way. Then he had led the slaughter of half of the Scarbutts. As well as skinning their mounts to make wolf skulls as trophies,until he finally found the offending rider.

Once caught he pinned Gurt Scarbutt down, urinated all over him, then, honour satisfied, with a wake of destruction behind his Buga's. ReelBad shrugged, gave the nod to his boyz, declared the war over and took the Buga's back to their home caves.

Not without a few skirmishes on the way back of course, but that was just for fun and not serious war business.

As ReelBadBugga stormed into the cave mouth, the runt goblin he had kicked was crawling back over the ledge grinning with relief at averting his fall down the mountainside and therefore his demise. He was just dusting himself off when two more of his hooded brethren came pirouetting out of the cave, having been unfortunate enough to be in the Buga's way. The collision of green flesh and black robes tumbled backwards over the rim. RellBigBuga would have probably smiled had he heard the screams and satisfying splats that brought them to an end.

The caves were dark and full of green foul smelling smoke. It would be enough to bring tears to the eyes of full-grown men. Orks are not, however, hampered by tear ducts. Evolution never saw the need to equip Orks to weep, for some reason beating other Orks to death with any available object was it seems a more viable survival trait.

In the caves, the rats sauntered in corners, too stoned on the vile green fumes to scurry. Mushrooms of every size and shape grew in the dank dripping caves, fields of them in the lower levels. In some places, a spaced-out goblin would be chewing happily while one of his kin was arguing with a rock which refused to let him past into '*the wooden stick for hunting in the dark.*'

At least that is what ReelBadBuga assumed the goblin was referring to when he said nightclub.

Reel ignored the minions of the goblin caves and bellowed "I Iz Hezes Mush wadda ya want. " with his customary gusto.

A runt in a black cowl pulling a runt squig on a leash that was no bigger than Reel's foot came scampering up. "Mushmuncha says to follow me, Oh, Mighty Warragg leader." He simpered, which impressed Reel, he didn't actually lead a Warragg, but liked the sound of the 'Oh mighty'.

Indeed, he was so busy considering the sound of 'Oh Mighty' he failed to hear the goblin append his statement with a whispered " yer fat oaf."

He grunted, "Lead on ya Runty goit-fetter." Resisting the urge to swat the little goblin but only because he thought it would be beneath him as an 'Oh Mighty' to do his own swatting of the runts. Somewhere in the back of his not particularly large mind, he considered for a moment if not being able to do your own swatting was going to be a major downside to the whole 'Oh Mighty' thing.

He liked swatting things…

He grunted once more and fell in behind the runt goblin who was scurrying along as fast as he was able, more dragging, than leading his pet squig in his wake.

They progressed downward into the heart of the runt goblin's mountain realm. Reel was surprised how busy it was, he had not been aware there were so many of the little runts in the caves. He suspected this may be due to a lack of good swatting, and absently tried to rectify this error with any of them that came in range of his hands. Somewhere in what we shall still call for the sake of argument, the back of his mind, a decision had been reached.

'Oh Mighty's could do their own swatting if they wanted to'

This was possibly the most impressive piece of abstract thinking ReelBadBuga had ever managed. So swat he did.

The caves teamed with activity which mostly seemed to revolve around growing and harvesting mushrooms, making stuff from mushrooms and trying to teach the not so tame spiders not to eat the mushrooms.

There were also groups of goblins trying to train spiders for riding. A process which seemed to involve as many goblins as possible. So that eventually the spider was so overfed it gave up eating, and then one of the goblins could get on the beast to ride it around.

Why anyone would ride anything that wasn't a boar escaped Reel, but then quite a lot did.

Finally, they arrived at a small cavern on the edge of a subterranean lake, where three goblins manned a raft, with long poles. And the runt with the squig clambered on board.

Reel did not trust the raft, or the goblins, or the water much, and any lake in the middle of a mountain was bound to have big albino flesh-eating fish in it.

But 'Oh Mighty' isn't scared of water, as he told himself and so he climbed aboard the ill-made raft which sunk further into the water. Much to the alarm of the good ship's crew, one of which was sent flying into the water where he scrambled for shore before the killer albino flesh eating tuna got him.

Progress across the lake was slow, mostly due to the nervous nature of the crew, and the rocking of the raft caused ReelBadBuga to experience seasickness for the first time. Which led to him decorating the deck at one point. Finally, though they reached a small rocky island in the middle of the lake. There sat the wizened old shaman, next to a large cauldron bubbling with a green mixture which smelled suspiciously like split pea soup.

ReelBadBuga hated split pea soup.

"Sit with me Oh Mighty one." The Shaman croaked. "It is time to learn your destiny," he said this with all due ominousness and a hiccup. Green fumes escaped his mouth when he did so.

"Glod has ceased fighting the humans gods in the sky to tell me of his mighty son who must unify the tribes."

"Whoz this then. Coz if anyone is leading a Warragg it will be me not some mighty son, Buga's lead Buga's not follow" ReelBadBuga grunted, swatting one of the boat crew who got too close.

The smoky atmosphere of the caves was making him nauseous, he longed for good proper smoke. Like the smoke from the corpses of his enemies, their tents smouldering after a raid. Rather than the vile green smoke which was giving him a bad head. Which I could claim was worsening his temper, but that would imply it could worsen form its default setting of raging.

"But, you are the mighty son of Glod, You Reel-BigBugga are the one who must lead us all in the mighty Warragg. For Glod has spoken to me in dreams. We must go east into the lands of the elves and the rat men. For they fight a war and have invited us not. The gods have chosen you RellBadBuga to lead us in this war… With of course my advice, Oh mighty one" the Shaman intoned with suitable dramatic menace, despite odd hiccup and a giggling fit.

ReelBadBuga's mind, if we have to call it that, was filled with visions of glorious battles, of the great sea of green descending on the non-green and having a really good axe up. Which is more or less like a punch up, but with weapons, and more fatal outcomes.

A Warrraggg with him at the head. Riding hard on his warboar. The thrill of the fight, the kill, the drinking afterwards and then the fights between your own side over who got to piss on the biggest of the slain…

Good times…

Tales to be told around the campfire for generations, his name above all others as the mighty Warragg leader.

So much was BigBadBuga enraptured by this heady vision of violent excess, he did not hear the shamans final words…

"And I'll get me some nice warp-stone chunks while everyone's busy fighting you big oaf then I'll be in charge, hiccup."

The next day at the top of the mountain the cry went out…

"WARRAGGGGGGGGGGGG!!!!!!!!"

And echoed across the valley of the nineteen tribes. Many were called, all answered…

Though not without a little fighting amongst themselves.

THE END

But if you want more to read… Turn the page…

The Hannibal Smyth Misadventures Series

A Spider In the Eye

From Russia With Tassels (coming summer 2019)

A Scar of Avarice (novella)

A Squid on the Shoulder (coming 2020)

Other Novels

Passing Place: Location Relative

Cider Lane: Of Silences and Stars

Also features in the following Anthologies

Harvey Duckman presents vol 1

ABOUT THE AUTHOR

Mark writes novels that often defy simple genre definitions, they could be described as speculative fiction, though Mark would never use the term as he prefers not to speculate.

When not writing novels Mark is a persistent pernicious procrastinator, he recently petitioned parliament for the removal of the sixteenth letter from the Latin alphabet.

He is also 7th Dan Blackbelt in the ancient Yorkshire marshal art of EckEThump and favours a one man one vote system but has yet to supply the name of the man in question.

Mark has also been known to not take bio very serious.

Email: darrack@hotmail.com

Twitter: @darrackmark

Blog: https://markhayesblog.com/

Printed in Great Britain
by Amazon